THE SECRET OF THE SAUCERS

OF THE

SAUCERS

Ned Daniels

The Secret of the Saucers

Copyright © 2025 Ned Daniels

Produced and printed by Stillwater River Publications. All rights reserved. Written and produced in the United States of America. This book may not be reproduced or sold in any form without the expressed, written permission of the author(s) and publisher.

Visit our website at **www.StillwaterPress.com** for more information.

First Stillwater River Publications Edition

ISBN: 978-1-965733-19-6

Library of Congress Control Number: 2024927075

1 2 3 4 5 6 7 8 9 10

Publisher's Cataloging-in-Publication
Provided by Cassidy Cataloguing Services, Inc.

Names: Daniels, Ned, author.
Title: The secret of the saucers / Ned Daniels.
Description: First Stillwater River Publications edition. | West
    Warwick, RI, USA : Stillwater River Publications, [2025] | Interest
    grade level: 5-8.
Identifiers: ISBN: 978-1-965733-19-6 | LCCN: 2024927075
Subjects: LCSH: Unidentified flying objects—Juvenile fiction. | Boats
    and boating—California—Juvenile fiction. | Santa Catalina Island
    (Calif.)—Juvenile fiction. | CYAC: Unidentified flying objects—
    Fiction. | Boats and boating—California—Fiction. | Santa Catalina
    Island (Calif.)—Fiction. | LCGFT: Science fiction. | Action and
    adventure fiction.
Classification: LCC: PZ7.1.D3125 Se 2025 | DDC: [Fic]--dc23

Written by Ned Daniels.
Cover and interior design by Elisha Gillette.
Published by Stillwater River Publications, West Warwick, RI, USA.

PLEASE READ THIS BEFORE
READING THE BOOK! PLEASE

Throughout the book I have used facts and events related to unidentified anomalous phenomenon (UAPs). Four of the five main characters—Stuart, Kate, Grammy, and Myrtle—use actual UAP facts in their dialogue, facts about UAPs I researched for this book. Masaneka DOES NOT use actual UAP facts as she is from the fictional land of Atlantis.

In the very last chapter however, Stuart and Myrtle use facts that are NOT factual, but it was a good way to end the story!

Have fun learning in a fun way about UAPs.

The author!

P.S. I have a bibliography at the end of the book, and all the references listed there contained the facts I used for this book.

Early June
Late Afternoon
At Kate's

Knock, Knock, Knock
     "Why mother, who could that be?" Kate asked in a mocking tone.

"I have only one answer, and that would be an ET!" Kate's mom, Myrtle, humorously said back.

To which Kate replied in a mocking tone of voice, "I fear you are right Mom." And with that she went to the door and opened it.

"Good afternoon young lady," Stuart said with an actor's sweep of his hand as he bowed. "What a pleasure to see you again!"

"Mom, it's not an ET, it's a Stuart!"

"Whaaaat?" came Stuart's reply.

"Well invite him in!"

"So good to see you my friend," Kate said in an earnest tone of voice.

"Thank you both, but what's with the," Stuart made air quotes, "ET reference?"

"Mom told me today that she heard from Dr. Fuller that you are back working at the think tank place up the street heading towards Falmouth."

"Yes, I got to Woods Hole late last night by train from NYC, and I didn't want to bother you guys, so I visited with Grammy at her house where I'll be staying again for the summer, and then I hit the sack!

"And guess what? I'm to work at researching UAPs, or their full and correct name, Unidentified Anomalous Phenomena! UAP is the correct acronym instead of UFO. The acronym UAP was created in 2022 by the Department of Defense. The 'F' in UFO stood for the word 'flying,' and that is no longer accurate. You see, the navy said that they've seen UAPs in the water, on the water, and coming out of the water with no sign of an exhaust!" Stuart paused, his voice going up in tone. "So, not all sightings were 'flying.' So, the navy convinced the feds to change it to UAPs.

"The United States government is concerned about the potential threat UAPs present to the people of Earth on land, sea, and air."

Kate's mom entered the living room and said in a stunned tone of voice, "You are serious about what you said about UAPs sighted in the oceans?"

"Yup."

"That's a bit frightening, isn't it?"

Kate quickly interjected, "No, that's very scary. The no exhaust part I mean. And could Masaneka and the people formerly of Atlantis have seen such things?" Kate asked, looking at Stuart.

"She is high on my list of people with whom to speak. And there's more I've already read about just today! As I began to take notes on all I read it seemed even more scary than I thought it would be."

"Look Stuart," Myrtle said, "since you're already surprised by what you've learned in one day, and since you're staying at your grandmother's, why don't you call her and invite her over for dinner? Then we can all hear what you've learned."

"Sounds good," Stuart said as he took out his cell phone and called his grandmother.

15 Minutes Later
A Knock on the Door Startled Everyone

A loud knock startled the three of them and they jumped anxiously.

"It's probably Grammy. I'll get the door." Kate's mom went to open it.

"Hi Grammy," Myrtle said as they hugged.

Stuart, now standing, said, "Come sit over here Grammy. I just started talking about my new job and all I've learned in one day!"

"Gladly Stuart." And with that she sat down on the chair beside him.

"Continue with your new knowledge sharing while I get dinner ready," Myrtle said as she headed for the kitchen. "I'll leave the door open so I can hear you."

"Well," Stuart said as he sat up straight in his

chair, "one of the most interesting places in the USA for UAPs is Catalina Island off the coast of California. They've experienced numerous UAP sightings as well as other anomalies at Santa Monica Bay near Catalina, and lately they're having more of these unusual sightings. And I have a small travel budget to go there and speak with people who have had such sightings and experiences related to these UAPs."

"That sounds so exciting Stuart!" Grammy said very proudly.

"But I'd like to ask you Grammy, Kate, Myrtle," he said in a raised voice so Myrtle would hear him in the kitchen, "to go with me!"

Myrtle walked into the living room and answered in a loud voice, "Sign us up Stuart!"

"And sign me up as well!" Grammy shouted.

"I am loving this summer, and it just began!" Kate said happily. "Thanks Mom for going along with this! This is what summer should be like! And maybe Masaneka could come as well!"

"Absolutely Kate! She's on my list," Stuart said back.

Myrtle, standing near the kitchen door said, "Wow! Things are moving fast, just like a UAP!" She giggled.

The others in the room just looked at her with open mouths.

"Too early for such a joke?" Myrtle said. "My boo-boo! So, if I offer you dinner, will you all forgive my enthusiasm?"

"For a fine dinner," Stuart replied, "you bet!"

"Good," Myrtle replied. "The timer is set, so when it goes off, we eat!"

"So, Stuart, given that you have a lot to share with us about Catalina, let's hear what you know." With that Myrtle turned to Grammy and Kate. "How does that sound ladies?"

Both Grammy and Kate chimed in at the same time. "It sounds good!"

"What I have about Catalina will be brief but interesting. But the next part will really startle you," he added.

"You're on Stu!" Kate blurted out.

"I'll start off by saying that the island is a hot spot for UAPs. It has a magnetic vortex that seems to 'relax' people who explore the island. One of the tour boats has a woman who leads the tour, and people really like her. We'll get on a tour with her. She'll share UAP sightings experienced on Catalina as well as those in the area surrounding the island. Some of what she shares may be frightening, but it will also be intriguing and fascinating.

"The full name of the island is Santa Catalina Island. The sightings on the island, in the water, and in areas around California have been going on for decades.

"Sightings have been in the air and underwater, and that's why I want to see if Masaneka can give me anything on those underwater observations.

"These sightings have been made by citizens, navy personnel on and off navy ships, and by sea-going vessels of sizes ranging from a small boat to massive ships that cross oceans and seas with tons of cargo and more. And all these sightings have happened over a very long period."

"During all this time was there any firing of weapons?" Kate asked.

"The only incident of firing from a UAP was in South America, and I just came across that reference this afternoon; I don't know any more about it," Stuart concluded.

"Sightings have been made in the air and underwater, and that's why I want to see if Masaneka can give me anything she has on those underwater observations.

"These sightings have been made by citizens, Navy personel on and off Navy ships, and by sea-going vessels of sizes from a small boat to major sized ships that cross oceans and seas with tons of cargo and more. And all these sightings have happened over a very long period."

"So, except for that example of firing of weapons that happened in South America, could they be here for peaceful or scientific reasons?" Kate asked.

"Good point Kate. For some time, the militaries of many countries, and that's including the USA, have prepared for the possibility of an attack, just to be ready in case such a thing happens."

"Have they prepared any strategy should the UAP occupants indicate that they are here for scientific reasons, and that they have technology and resources to share for the good of the people of Earth?" Kate questioned.

"Good point Kate," her mom interjected. "I've been wondering the same thing as they don't seem to have done anything that was aggressive or that used weapons."

"I like that idea, and I think I'm going to raise it in the conclusion of my first report," Stuart shared in a softer tone of voice. He raised his hand and pointed at Kate. "Thank you Kate and Mom for that idea. It's powerful, and it must be raised as an issue and planned for accordingly." With that Stuart made some notes, and the others just looked on, nodding in agreement.

"Okay," he began, before Mom interrupted with

"Could we stop now as the timer just went off, so dinner is ready."

"Sounds good," said Grammy. "Is this okay with you Stu?"

"It sure is as I'm starving!"

With that they all headed into the kitchen.

After Dinner
The Details of UAPs on Catalina are Startling

"That was a delicious meal Myrtle, and thank you for inviting me," Grammy said. Everyone nodded in agreement. Grammy then turned her head to her grandson. "What's next Stu?"

"I'd like to start with some early sightings off the coast of Catalina, and then go into a big picture of other sightings and what the USA is doing related to them. Okay?"

Everyone nodded without saying a word.

"An early sighting that happened many years ago and which began to get the needed attention of the government involved three army veterans. In July of 1949, three army veterans sighted a flying object over the island. The sighting was a flying saucer. It hovered for a short time. Then it flew off. Its speed was greater than any military aircraft at that time or since. That speed was such that no human could have survived it if they were a passenger in that UAP. With that sighting and with others, it became clear that the government had to do something.

"Other sightings of UAPs started to be investigated by the military and the government of the USA, something other countries were already doing.

"The UAPs moved at phenomenal speeds and at hundreds of miles per hour. They could accelerate at amazingly fast speeds unlike any flying machine on this earth! And as I said earlier, no human on Earth could survive at such a speed. They could change directions in a split second, and again, no visible exhaust fumes. And they could stop on a dime as well!

"Overall, ninety to ninety-five percent of the UAP sightings could be proven to be false and be of manmade objects or other earth-based things such as weather balloons, birds reflecting the sun just right, and small planes far from the observer doing tricks in the air. And actual military planes and other military flying objects were often the sources of sightings later proved to be false."

Stuart paused and took a sip of water.

"I love this one! A pilot thought he saw a UAP.

With that the pilot and copilot agreed to go back and look again. You know what they saw?" Stuart asked.

"No," was the answer back from the three ladies in the room.

"What they saw when they flew back was a Bart Simpson balloon!"

Kate, Myrtle, and Grammy looked at each other and groaned.

Stuart roared.

"I'm sorry, but I just had to share that. And now I'll get back to being serious." He cleared his throat and began again.

"The remaining five percent or so of UAP sightings could not be validated as manmade, and one thing that very much supported that was the very rapid speed and maneuvers with which they could initiate and change direction, all with little or no sound."

With that Stuart stopped and took another sip of water.

In a soft and puzzled voice Grammy asked, "And all this Stuart is just the beginning of the sightings offshore and onshore that have been documented?"

"Yes, Grammy, that is correct. And I haven't begun to share details of sightings.

"The military agreed that they could not

conclusively state the exact origin of these UAPs; however, they did conclusively state that the origin of these sighted aircraft phenomena was not from somewhere on Earth, but instead from outside of our solar system.

"What's even more scary is that such sightings have been observed and written down over the span of many centuries."

With that Stuart took another sip of water and walked to the bathroom.

"Well, ladies," Myrtle stated, "this is proving to be a most interesting night! Yikes!"

Stuart returned from the bathroom and sat in his chair.

Grammy proudly patted his arm.

He looked over at her and smiled. "And I haven't even begun to share most of what I've studied today."

"Wow Stuart. How can there be more?" Kate said in a strong voice.

"I've barely scratched the surface. And I've yet to ask Masaneka to come on board and help me, and, well, I'd also like to ask you if you'd help me with the research Kate. Your idea about having a strategy for a peaceful arrival of these people has not popped up in any of my readings so far, so that's big, and I plan to make it a strongly worded statement in my closing remarks."

"What would you want me to do? I know nothing about this topic."

"I was thinking about you researching the foreign UAP sightings that are documented and taking brief notes on each. I have plenty of materials. Would you do that?"

Mom suddenly spoke up. "I'd like to work with Kate on this. My interest has been piqued by what you've shared so far."

Mom turned to Kate and asked, "Would you mind if I worked with you?"

"Not at all!!"

"Great, then it's settled," Stu said.

And then Grammy chimed in, "I want to do some research as well, but what has made me most interested is the unique qualities about these UAPs. I'd just like to capture all the key words and phrases about speed, no exhaust, sharp and very quick turns, etc. I'd do a chart with dates and locations and any attributes of these specific sightings. Would that be okay?"

"Absolutely! But I'd like you to only focus on sightings over the United States. Okay?"

"Got it Stuart," Grammy replied. "Got it!"

"Again, another idea that will add depth and

breadth to my final report. Wow!" Stuart happily shouted out.

"I'll call Masaneka now to see if she can make it, for, let's say, nine thirty tomorrow? Okay?

"But in closing, and on a more serious note, pilots did, and to a degree, still do fear a stigma will be attached to them if they say they saw something. The government is now making it clear that all suspicious sightings should be reported even if it turns out to be Bart Simpson!" And then he roared in laughter.

Saturday Morning Meeting with Masaneka

Stuart got a good night's sleep, and slowly crawled out of bed. *What is this day going to be like?* he said to himself. And with that he went into the bathroom to shower and shave and to get ready for the day.

At the same time Grammy was cooking a light breakfast of bacon and eggs with a piece of toast. She whistled while she worked and had a big smile on her face. "What a day this one is going to be," she muttered to herself.

"Good morning, Grammy. What's for breakfast?"

"Your favorite, bacon and eggs with a slice of toast."

"Yum!"

After breakfast Stuart and Grammy drove over to Kate and Myrtle's.

"Great!" Stuart barked out. "That's Masaneka's car, so we can start right away."

"Let's visit first Stu, and then we can get started. You haven't seen Masaneka for many months," Grammy suggested.

"It's just that I'm so excited about how much support I've gotten from you, Kate, and Myrtle. And now Masaneka."

They pulled up in front of Kate's home, turned off the motor, and got out of the car.

"I'm so excited. I feel like I'm going to explode," Stuart said as he all but hopped out of the car.

"That's a good thing!" Grammy laughed back at him. "Now hustle up there and ring the doorbell!"

He hustled up to the door and did just that.

Then the door opened a crack, and a voice came out saying, "What galaxy are you from?"

At first, Stuart was startled.

Grammy was now at his side. "What's the problem?"

"Someone inside just asked me what galaxy I'm from. Too funny."

"Tell them you're from a galaxy far, far away."

"But it's just Kate busting me."

Grammy leaned over and whispered in his ear, "Say that again in a very deep voice. Then I'll quietly open the screen door and rattle it. That'll teach them!"

Suddenly Grammy rattled the screen door real hard.

Stuart took his cue and said in a deep falsetto voice, "We are from a galaxy hundreds of light-years away. Let us in."

Laughter came from the crack in the door, and then it opened as Kate and Masaneka stood there laughing.

"Come in, come in. After such a long trip you must be tired," came Kate's voice.

Masaneka then jokingly said, "Please be more specific as to how many light-years away."

"Alright you," Stuart said. "Three! So, let's get this show on the road."

Kate opened the door and Stuart and Grammy entered.

Myrtle was standing there with a big smirk on her face. "Grammy," she said with that big grin still on her face, "let's hope things are more serious than this as we meet today. Oh, and I prepared a cup of coffee for you." And with that she offered Grammy her cup of coffee on a saucer.

"I sure hope so, and thanks for the coffee," Grammy said back with a big grin on her face.

Stuart leaned over and gave Masaneka a big hug. "Thanks for coming."

"I'm glad to be here as Kate told me about why you wanted me, and I was stunned. When Atlantis existed under Sao Miguel or as we now call it, Saint Michael's Island in the Azores, we had encounters with strange people in what you call flying saucers which we called plates."

"Plates?" Stuart questioned with a grin on his face.

"Yes." And with that Masaneka got up and took Myrtle's coffee saucer and Grammy's as well. "Watch," she said, and she put one plate upside down, on top of the bottom plate. "See, they're plates."

Everyone laughed.

"There were six of us riding our dolphin horses. We had just found about twenty gold coins in an old shipwreck, and when we went around a rock outcropping, we saw one of the plates. One of our riders tapped it. Then suddenly a wall opened, and there they were, three of them, standing and looking at us but showing no emotion. We didn't verbally communicate with them, but we did wave at them. They seemed very perplexed by us."

"You mean you've made contact with them?!" Stuart blasted out in a loud, questioning voice.

"Yes, but please don't yell."

"I'm sorry, but this is exactly what I was hoping for, and that was with the people of Atlantis and why they might have seen the flying 'plates,'" Stuart said as he finger-quoted 'plates.' Stuart took a deep breath. "This blows my mind! Is there anything else to share with us?"

"Yes, she replied, "we made a gesture of offering the gold coins to them. They looked at the coins, but only their eyes moved. Then they seemed to speak, and suddenly a very small door under the saucer opened and a robotic arm came out to my friend who had the gold coins. He put them in the plate-like endpiece of this robotic arm, and it went back in, and the little door shut."

No one said a word. They were just sitting there, imagining what Masaneka had just described.

"And as we watched the three aliens, another small door behind them opened and a saucer-like dish came out of the wall with the gold coins. They looked at them and then shut the wall of the plate, or saucer as you call it, and then all we saw was the outside of the saucer."

After that the five of them sat silently in the living room.

Stuart was shaking his head in shock.

Myrtle then spoke. "Grammy, would you like another cup of coffee?"

"Yes, I would," she said in a stunned voice. "Yes, I would."

"I'll heat up another pot now." Myrtle went into the kitchen.

She came back a few minutes later with a tray of donuts and a pot of coffee. She then turned to Grammy. "Here's a pot of coffee Grammy when you're ready, and for you kids there are donuts!" she said with her voice going up as she emphasized the word 'donuts.'

"We had nothing like this in Atlantis," Masaneka shared as she looked at the donut. "I'm still having to slowly eat any food served on the surface of Earth, as my digestive system is not used to all this stuff. But donuts are high on my list of things I really like!"

The kids each took a donut, and Grammy and Myrtle looked on with smiles.

Stuart took a bite of his donut and started to speak.

"Stuart," Grammy said in a firm voice, "finish your donut before you talk."

He swallowed and said, "Sorry Grammy."

Grammy nodded in return.

"Masaneka, why do you think the aliens were perplexed?"

"Well, we were on our dolphin horses, we had our hair woven into the frames harnessed to our bodies, and we, well, we just tapped the saucer and then a wall opened, and we waved. Wouldn't you be perplexed if you saw something like that for the first time?"

"For sure!" Stuart answered back. "May I ask you some more questions?"

"Of course," she answered.

"First, did they wave back, and what did they look like?"

"One sort of waved back as if it didn't know what to do. They were very tall, but remember the people of Atlantis, like me, are all very short. They sort of looked like us but were thin and very tall, and the three of them looked almost like triplets, and their hair was very closely cut."

"Our soldiers have haircuts like that starting in boot camp. Were they in uniforms?"

"I think so, but we were so stunned at seeing them that I don't recall." She paused. "Wait, they did have a tight fitting outfit on that was almost the color of them. There was a seam down the middle of the uniform. I remember that now."

"What color were they?" Kate asked

"I think they were a light brown."

"What else was in the room they were in?" Stuart asked.

"All I could see behind them was a dull gray wall, and nothing else. They were standing, and the wall that opened went from the floor to the ceiling, and they were just a few inches short of the ceiling. Oh," she added, "the window was the same shape as the plate, I mean saucer."

Grammy, with a very perplexed voice asked, "You said that you did not see anything behind them, right?"

"Yes, just a dull gray wall."

Grammy turned to Stuart and asked, "How would they fly it?"

"That's the million-dollar question, and all I can think of is that the gauges were in another part of the plate," Stuart said with a chuckle.

"How long did you look at them?" Kate asked.

"Maybe a minute or two, and then the wall closed. We rode around the plate and then left," Masaneka said.

"Do you have any other encounter stories to tell us about?" Myrtle asked.

"Yes, I do. Atlanteans saw other plates but only a few opened the door to look at us. The other stories I've heard were basically the same. The aliens never came out of their plate, and other than a wave story now and then, there's nothing I can offer other than an opinion given what we've talked about so far and that is that they knew there were humans on the surface of Earth, but they probably did not know about the Atlanteans who lived in the ocean. Plus, we thought that the plates were made by you who lived on the surface, not aliens from another galaxy!"

"That sounds very probable Masaneka. What you shared is amazing and validates that they've been here before, and it makes me question if they live in a planet of just water as they seemed to know how to land their plates in oceans." Stuart paused. "I think we need to use the term saucer, not plates, if that's alright with you Masaneka," he said.

"Of course," she said back. And then, "Wait! I bet my grandfather, King, will have much more to share. I'll call him in Portugal tomorrow morning."

"Excellent!" Stuart said.

And to everyone Myrtle said, "Please come into the kitchen for a light breakfast."

After a Light Breakfast

Grammy walked in first from the kitchen, followed by Masaneka and Stuart who were chatting amiably, and finally Kate and her mom.

Stuart then began, "First, Myrtle, thanks for the donuts and for breakfast. Very good! It's my second breakfast today!"

Myrtle replied quickly, "It was my pleasure."

Stuart nodded, and then began.

"Masaneka will be contacting King tomorrow for as much as she can get in the way of information on any sighting by the Atlanteans when they once lived under the island of Saint Michael's in the Azores before coming to live on land in Portugal, their original home centuries ago," he paused, "and then I'd like to share a few more examples before going over what I'd like Kate and Myrtle to do and what

I'd like Grammy to do. Then I think we're finished for the day as a group. Plus, I must get to my job!"

"Sounds good," said Kate.

"And I agree as well," said Myrtle.

"Well, I guess I'll get my two cents worth in now to give you all an idea I have for a chart that will be a grid of just key words, dates, objects sighted, et cetera," Grammy shared. "I already have taken a few notes based on what Stuart has said and what Masaneka has said. All of that and more will allow me to determine the best headings and their order, with dates and locations as the first two column headings of my chart. I see that as the only absolute data before investigations, if any are or have been done, and that's where I am right now. I will fill each space of input by the date and location of the sighting or the encounter. This way we'll begin to see patterns."

"I like that," Myrtle said, as everyone else nodded in agreement.

Stuart said to her quickly and in a most pleased voice, "Wow, Grammy, that kind of grid would make it easy for people to see the critical details immediately. But please just focus on sightings in the United States."

Grammy nodded with a smile on her face.

"Let me get started now, and I think this will be

an interesting way to finish this meeting, and it will give you an idea of the range of locations, sightings, encounters, and more with just a few examples. And then we'll be on our way as I must get to my desk at work and start further research; I'll also share how our group will proceed."

"UAPs have been sighted just about every place in the world, and" he looked at Masaneka, "even in the oceans."

"Oh, that will be another heading on my chart: land, air, and then oceans!" Grammy shouted out.

"Excellent Grammy. And now, let me begin with a bunch of examples of sightings that will give you a broad concept of what we'll end up with.

"These UAP sightings have been happening all over the world, and in some cases for long periods of time and in other cases just singular sightings. Something about our nuclear plants also seems to be a factor in numerous sightings; guess they're of interest to extraterrestrials. And there was a two-year episode of such sightings where the sightings were numerous, but with only one interaction, and you'll laugh when I get to it!

"These two years of sightings happened in Belgium starting in 1989. Hovering, triangular objects were sighted numerous times over about a two-year period. And keep in mind what I said, about saucers versus 'plates.'" He looked at Masaneka as he finger-quoted the last word.

"In one instance—you'll get a kick out of this encounter—a large triangular UAP was hovering near a road one evening. A driver and his wife, seeing it and the very bright light it was making, flashed his car lights at the UAP. And this is the funny encounter—the UAP flashed its lights back at the driver.

"The authorities weren't sure what to make of this encounter with the triangular saucer and with the man and his wife in their car when it was shared by the driver later, but it sure got some chuckles. But we must ask, given that form of communication, and if it was a sign of communication, was it a friendly one or just a coincidence?

"After these sightings and others had been seen and reported, people, including police, well-educated citizens, and others, were now less reluctant to share their encounters or observations. The people felt more confident about notifying government officials about UAP sightings because they would not be ridiculed as people had once been when these encounters occurred.

"Very credible photographs were taken in 1958 in Brazil by a senior military officer. These photos validated the existence of UAPs, then referred to as UFOs.

"Our American pilots and navy personnel and their foreign counterparts were at first reluctant to share observations for the same reason: they might get ridiculed. But now with so many sightings, military of all ranks and levels are coming forward and not fearing ridicule.

"Again, in Brazil in 1986, sightings, radar capture, and photographs of these UAPs were taken. They observed UAPs very quickly accelerating, decelerating, hovering, making very sharp turns, and accelerating at very fast speeds, faster than any jet we had on Earth, but from a hovering position. And as I said earlier, a human could not endure and live at such rapid speeds of acceleration.

"But again, it was the military officers and the pictures that validated their existence and that gave the sightings credibility.

"A question was raised as to whether they were manned by aliens or by some form of artificial intelligence, also referred to as AI. In fact, another question was whether the UAPs seen in the air, on the ground, on water, or in the water, were coming from a mothership that was, if it existed, not detected by any of our land, sea, or air technology. Also raised as a question was whether we might contact alien creatures that are robots, not live creatures, as a robot could survive rapid acceleration, but probably not a living creature.

"This is my last story, and then we'll consider the next steps, and when we can meet again.

"At another sighting in Brazil a short time later, people observed twenty-one UAPs. So, we can say with confidence that the people of Brazil and their military share confidence in the validity of these sightings, and they had the proof to support these observations!"

Stuart finished with, "And that's all I have to say at this time!"

"Well Stuart, that was a lot. If I go back to my concern about them coming possibly for peace, these noncombative encounters currently show no use of weapons or killing technologies," Kate said.

"A very good observation Kate."

Then he blurted out, "And now, assignments! Yeah!"

The four looked at Stuart, shook their heads, and then laughed!

"Masaneka, you'll contact King for details on any UAP encounters by the Atlanteans. Grammy, you'll put together a model of a grid to capture key points, not lengthy sentences. Kate and Myrtle, you'll begin research on USA sightings. When I get back to my desk, I'll do further research on encounters elsewhere in the world."

"Sounds good Stu, and you've done a great job this morning giving us context for what we may read about and what to capture in the way of words and key points," Myrtle said. "Well done!"

Stu sort of blushed.

"Thanks for hosting Myrtle, and thanks for breakfast," Grammy said.

"And I'm going to try donuts again," Masaneka said with a big smile.

"I'll join you when you do Masanka!" Kate blurted out.

"I can't wait to get started Stu, and thanks to all of you for coming." Myrtle then asked, "Should we plan to meet here tomorrow once Masaneka hears from King, and you get back to us?"

"I'll call each of you with our meeting time tomorrow."

And with that Grammy, Stuart, and Masaneka headed for the door. As Grammy put her hand on the doorknob, she turned to Myrtle and said, "Thanks for your wonderful hospitality!!"

Assignment Sharing
Three in the Afternoon

"Thanks again for supporting me in my new assignment. What you are doing will help me, but I'll also be getting your opinions as well as your insight and phrasing, all of which I can use as I write my report. So, thanks again, very much."

He turned to Kate and said, "I mentioned to my boss your suggestion that they may be coming in peace, not war, and he liked that idea, especially when I shared the encounters with the Atlanteans and the light flashing from a car to a saucer and back; you know, the one in Belgium.

"But first, I'd like to share how our meeting could proceed, and then we'll begin. And again, Kate and Myrtle, thank you for hosting, and do my eyes see a snack on the coffee table?" Stuart hungrily and humorously said.

"Yes, Stuart, they're healthy and delicious, and they're called protein balls," Myrtle replied. "Everyone, please help yourself."

And suddenly Kate, Grammy, Masaneka, and Stuart all reached for the protein balls and took one.

After one bite Stuart said, "Nectar of the gods!"

Everyone chuckled.

A minute later, after all had eaten this delicious snack, Stuart began again. "I'll start by sharing a few things I've learned from my morning's research, and then I'll ask Masaneka to share her conversation with King. Then Mrytle and Kate, I'd like you to take the floor, and we'll finish with Grammy as everything we share will be what she'll want for her chart. Any suggestions?" Stuart asked.

"Sounds like a plan," Kate said. "Let's get going!"

Stuart began, "One of the United States government's greatest concerns is that many of the sightings have been over nuclear power plants, nuclear subs, and nuclear ships, and that has raised many concerns. A two-year series of sightings over Belgium raised a lot more concerns until someone realized that it's the, so to speak, home to NATO, the North Atlantic Treaty Organization, headquarters, and how they would know something like that is a big question. There have also been numerous sightings, as I shared yesterday, over Catalina Island." Stuart paused for a sip of water. The others waited attentively.

"An interesting set of sightings took place in Nagasaki and Hiroshima, the locations of the atomic bombs the United States dropped to hopefully end Word War II, and I'm pretty sure those bombings did stop the war.

"But the only logical reasons they'd be sighted often over those two cities might be to discern the consequences of a nuclear bombing's effect some seventy-five years later. They probably studied the land and life where the bombs were dropped. But again, this is only speculation.

"And I have many other USA sightings, but I'll end on this one so we can hear from Masaneka.

"On of the most talked about areas in the USA for where strange things supposedly have happened, a place that a dead alien might be kept in and more, is Area 51, a hundred twenty miles northwest of Las Vegas, Nevada. The United States government keeps that area totally restricted as it is also a place where innovations in flying machines are made and for obvious reasons kept secret." Stuart paused. "So, as you can see, a lot of interest is out there, and obviously for good reason."

He turned to Masaneka, and said, "You're on Masaneka, and I can't wait to hear what you have to say!"

She gave a thumbs-up and got up. "After my conversation with Rei—I mean King! 'Rei' is the Portuguese word for 'king'; I was totally stunned. I shared here yesterday an earlier encounter with a flying plate as we called them, but from now on I'll use the term UAPs to be current. King was most interested in your work Stuart, and he'd like to be kept informed of your conclusions."

"Of course," Stuart replied. "I can't wait to hear what you have to say." And with that he reached for another protein ball.

Masaneka began. "Most of the encounters were like the one I described at our last meeting. What's different is that there have been many times when we've encountered numerous UAPs just sitting on one of the ledges below sea level under the sea off of Saint Michael's Island. Saint Michael's is on the top of an ocean mountain, and we in Atlantis thought they were from the people on the surface.

"And I agree with Kate that they may be coming in peace; however, the governments of the world should also be prepared for an invasion or an attack.

"After speaking with King, he surprised me with some of his stories. Some of his stories were like the one I shared with the gold as a gift. And if you didn't know, the people of Atlantis, before we came to the surface, salvaged over a period of hundreds of years a great amount of gold from ships that sank, ships that we could get to that weren't deeper than the depths of the ocean to which we could dive. King told me this morning that the gold they brought to the surface may be worth as much as seven hundred *million* in American dollars."

"Wow," said Grammy. "That's phenomenal!'

"Phenomenal beyond words," Stuart chimed in.

"That is just wonderful Masaneka," said Myrtle. "Does he have any plans for it?"

"None at this time, but he's thinking of splitting it among all the people of Atlantis who now live in Portugal, as well as to give a large sum to the National Azulejo Museum."

Kate sat there with her mouth open, and then she said, "What an incredible thing to have happened. Wow!"

Then Stuart said, "Okay, okay, let's get back to what King said about UAPs," as he turned to Masaneka.

"Yes, it is incredible, but so are the stories I'm about to share. The first story King told me was astonishing. On one dive about twenty feet down, the lead diver saw something and motioned the others to hug tight to the side of the mountain. He then went carefully around the rock outcropping the divers were hiding behind, and he saw over two hundred plate-shaped objects, what you call flying saucers. They were hovering tight to the mountain, and no sound was heard. Then, suddenly, they took off heading west towards the Americas. I think that they might have sighted our first diver when he went around the rock outcropping. And the strange thing was that with all those UAPs, there was no trail of bubbles or any wake of water or any sound."

"T-two hund-dred?" Stuart stammered. "Two hundred?"

"Yes," she replied, "at least two hundred. And when the others came around the rock outcropping they saw them leaving."

"Oh, my," Myrtle said softy. "That is a very scary thought—over two hundred!"

"As I said earlier, most of the sightings were like the first one I told you about.

"The second sighting I wanted to share was one the divers saw at night. Some of our, as you call them, teenagers, were diving one evening near the shore when they saw bright light in the water about a half mile away. They surfaced and talked about going to explore the source of the light. They agreed to proceed with caution, and went back into the water, going down about ten feet, but staying close to the ledge at the end of the beach where it dropped off very quickly. As they got closer, they could see that there were three UAPs, all saucer shaped, but with bright lights, and each set of lights was about twelve feet wide, with three for each of the saucer-shaped UAPs. One of the girls signaled to one of the boys to swim closer to the three saucers, and so they took off while the others stayed behind. As they got closer, the closest saucer turned its light towards them. The two kids stopped, and then they swam closer. When the girl put her hand over her eyes, the saucer immediately lowered the brightness of the light. The two of them waved at that saucer, and then it quickly flashed back with the softer light. That was it. The boy tapped the girl's shoulder and signaled to go back, and so they did."

"Unbelievable," Kate said as she shook her head. "The girl initiated the idea of going to the saucer!" She paused and then yelped, "Yes!"

"And that's all King could tell me as he was going to meet with the bank and with the government leaders of the Azores and of Portugal."

"No problem Masaneka, no problem," Stuart uttered softly. "I have notes of a sighting off the coast of California in 1992 where it was reported that more than two hundred disk-shaped objects were sighted in Santa Monica Bay. They hovered for a few minutes and then flew away at a rapid speed, and with not much more than a slight humming sound."

He looked at Masaneka. "I would suspect that what was seen at Santa Monica Bay, given the large number of saucers, may have been the same ones your friends saw when they were swimming."

Stuart turned to Grammy. "There's something for your chart."

"Believe me Stuart, I had already written both observations down with a question as to whether or not the sighting at Saint Michael's and at Santa Monica Bay were related." She turned to Masaneka. "Can you tell me in what year your adult divers saw the two hundred or so saucers and when the teenagers saw the three with the bright lights?"

"I didn't get that piece of information as we in Atlantis did not use the same year count as you do on the surface of Earth. I'll ask King the next time I speak with him if he knows how far back these encounters were."

Stuart nodded and said, "Okay."

"Let's have a light supper of sandwiches on the back deck. My mind is blown by Masaneka's stories," Myrtle said.

And they all got up and headed to the kitchen and on to the deck.

Back from Sandwiches
On the Back Deck

"Y|ou have a beautiful view from your deck Myrtle," Grammy said. "My view is of the backyard of my nice neighbors."

"My husband and I found it just before Kate was born, but sadly he died a few years later. And I still miss him."

"I was too young to remember him, but my favorite picture is of him lifting me in the air while Mom was looking on and smiling," Kate softly shared.

"Oh, I'm so sorry to hear that," Grammy told her and Myrtle.

"Thank you, but know that he's still in my thoughts and prayers," Myrtle softly shared as she turned to Kate. "But he had the joy of Kate as a baby, and that's one of my favorite memories."

"Memories are what much of life is about," Stuart offered, "just like the memories of the many people who have seen UAPs. But the memories you're sharing are much more beautiful than the scary memories people have of UAPs."

"For sure," Myrtle replied.

Everyone was quiet for a few seconds, and then Stuart spoke.

"As we go forward with our research, I'd like you to keep what we are doing secret, keep only the details that are specific to the categories on Grammy's chart, and any additional details that make the sightings significant. What has amazed me is how many related events and emotions were shared as a result of these sightings."

"That's good advice Stuart," Myrtle shared.

"Grammy would like to share with you what she has on her graph."

Date	Location	# Seen	Describe Shape	Estimated Speed
11/06/2006	O'Hare Airport	1	Disc, metallic, size estimates from 22' to 88'	rapid

"This is the first half of what I'm proposing currently. If a new column or two is needed, then I'll add it," Grammy stated. "As you can see, I've used the sighting at O'Hare as an example. As I do my research and as you give me examples for me to check against what I have, I'll insert them. I want to use the date as what will determine where each entry will go. That way we'll have a chronological listing.

"When Masaneka hears back from King I might do another chart just like this for her list of sightings. And if necessary, a third chart can be made for locations outside of the USA, maybe also ones for different countries, as there were so many sightings for Belgium.

"What's going to add value is when one chart has the same basic sighting as another chart. I think this will be the case when the Atlanteans saw two hundred UAPs, and then the same number of UAPs were seen coming out of the waters of Santa Monica Bay.

"Any more questions or suggestions?" Grammy scanned the room.

No one raised a question.

"Good." Then she paused. "I'll be using a different way of presenting my chart at our next meeting."

"What do you mean?" Kate asked.

"You'll see at my next presentation," Grammy said with a smile.

# of Turns	Hovered?	On Land	On or In Sea	In Air
0	Yes	No	No	Yes

"The second half may be a little harder to fill in in terms of number of turns as some may not be accurately recalled. In that case I'll use something like what I have here. The number lets the reader know that there was not an accurate count. Remember, some of the people who see a UAP may be stunned and therefore accuracy may be off. Any questions?"

Masaneka raised her hand. "So given the two hundred or so sighted by the Atlanteans, we can fill in the columns, but the date will be as close as I can make it once I speak with King, right?"

Grammy pondered Masaneka's reply. "Yes, that would be correct. And know that not every column may be filled in, and that's alright as it may not be relevant, or the observer of the UAP may not recall the specific information in question.

"Any more questions or suggestions?" Grammy scanned the room.

No one raised a question.

"Good, and now back to you Stuart."

"Thanks so much Grammy. And with that, I'd

like to close the meeting! And I'll email you tomorrow about our next meeting."

Big Surprises
At Stuart's Next Meeting

They were all together now in Kate and Myrtle's living room. After some small talk, Stuart slowly rose, scanning each of the faces in the room. He went quickly but with purpose. When he was standing up straight, he reached slowly and deliberately into his pocket and pulled out a small plastic candy dispenser. He then slowly walked to Grammy, then Myrtle, then Masaneka, and finally Kate.

Kate looked askance at him and took the candy. Stuart just stood there.

"It's a Tic Tac!" Kate blurted out. "Why all the drama?"

"An astute and probing question Katherine," he said, using Kate's full name. "Does anyone make a connection to the candy, the Tic Tac candy?" he said in a strange voice before pausing with an equally strange look on his face.

"The Nimitz!" Grammy blurted out!

"Very good Grammy. I see that you're doing your homework," he said, again in a strange and carefully modulated voice.

"Stuart, what's going on?" Grammy asked in a somewhat angry tone.

"Yeah, Stuart, what's with all the drama?" Kate asked.

"What's drama mean, Kate?" Masaneka asked.

"This is all too funny," Myrtle chuckled out. "Too funny."

Grammy intervened. "He's being overly dramatic, but appropriate with the Tic Tac reference. It was a sighting from two F/A-18 fighters who couldn't believe what they saw before flying back to the aircraft carrier the USS *Nimitz*. The *Nimitz*, contacted by the USS *Princeton*, a very advanced warship, had been asked by the *Princeton* to investigate a very puzzling radar sighting about thirty miles off the coast of Baja, Mexico. When the pilots approached the given location they saw, far below them, just above a very turbulent and frothy ocean, a stationary, egg-shaped object just hovering over the ocean. As the two pilots flew down and closer to this sight, they saw slight movements of the object, which the pilots thought indicated it was aware of their presence. Then suddenly, the object ascended at supersonic speed and disappeared." Grammy paused.

"The 'Tic Tac' name was used because it somewhat looked like a Tic Tac candy. Here's proof of the speed it could achieve." She took a deep breath. "A minute later the Tic Tac was detected sixty miles away. Wow!" And after another deep breath she added, "Technically it's not a USA sighting, which is the assigned range for my chart, but I read about it, and, well..." she looked at Stuart, "you finish the story, okay?"

"Thank you, Grammy, for that excellent explanation of what was sighted. And now to the Tic Tac!" he added with emphasis as he popped one into his mouth.

"An officer coined the name 'Tic Tac' because it looked like one—it was white and oblong in shape—and it had no wings, or other way to change direction." Stuart paused. "When the F/A-18 pilots returned to the aircraft carrier, they were greeted by their shipmates wearing aluminum hats meant to bust the pilots as these joking guys thought they were being funny! Well, it turns out that the F/A-18 pilots were not amused!

"As you can see by the last aluminum hat joke, early skepticism showed itself in weird ways. Today people are less apt to mock someone when they share a UAP sighting story.

"The irony," Stuart continued, "is that the Tic Tac incident was kept quiet for several years, but when the government finally acknowledged it, it became and has remained an important part of US history, and now tic tac is written as Tic Tac, with capital Ts."

"Got anymore Tic Tac candies Stuart?" Kate asked in a snobby tone of voice.

Shaking his head, Stuart replied by just walking over and popping one into her open hand.

Masaneka offered her own hand, and Stuart responded accordingly.

He then turned to Grammy and Myrtle and asked them politely as he glared at Kate, "Would one of you ladies like a Tic Tac?"

Both Grammy and Myrtle, chuckling, put up their hands and in unison said, "Thanks!"

He then stopped glaring at Kate and said, "Okay, let's get back to the purpose of the meeting!

"What I'm going to say now is my opinion as to why they might be seen here on Earth. Kate had raised the idea that maybe they are here for peace not conquest, and I feel that's a very logical position. Another thought is that maybe they have run out of some critical resource such as gold, and I say that because of the encounter Masaneka shared about her friends in Atlantis offering the gold coins. And again, this is strictly supposition."

Grammy then interjected with a big smile, "Maybe they're here to see if it would be a stop on a tour of the universe, and they need to know if their people could survive here for a possible visit." And with that she giggled! "But let me now be more serious with my opinion. Maybe they are so advanced that they don't have diseases, or wars, or random killings, or anything as evil as what we sometimes have here on Earth. I bet that they've solved such problems, and they are observing us to see if it's worth the effort and time to visit here." Then Grammy sat down.

"Wow," said Myrtle. "That is such a deep and powerful idea, and it could be a correct one. Let's hope it is, and if anything further happens with an actual face-to-face encounter, hopefully it will be peaceful."

The living room was silent for a few seconds as the five of them just pondered what Grammy said and Myrtle's reaction.

Masaneka raised her hand. "May I share a

possible reason for them coming here for their very short and possible frequent visits?"

Everyone nodded.

"Many of the sightings have been over water, on water, and in water. Clearly, they know what water is as they've used it very effectively. So, perhaps they come from a planet of water. Maybe they're looking to colonize. And maybe they took the gold coins because they just thought it was from other people who live in water, and it was a sign of welcome." Masaneka paused.

"Or could they be somehow connected to octopus?" Again, a pause.

"What?!" said Stuart.

"Octopus defy logic in terms of how they fit among the creatures of our oceans and seas, as well as creatures on land. Maybe they brought octopus here millions of years ago. Who knows?!" Masaneka stopped with an emphasis on her last sentence.

The room was silent.

"I'd like to add one more thought," Masaneka said, "and that is maybe they were exploring our waters to see if they could take some of our water for a need they have on their planet. Remember, the people of Atlantis have left the ocean and the city of Atlantis and its colonies because of ocean pollution, and because we needed our babies to live."

Silence filled the room.

Stuart, sitting now, spoke. "You have raised very rational questions as have Kate and Grammy about why they may have come here and then left so quickly. And your point, Masaneka, about the oceans and all the in, on, and over the ocean sightings we've recorded; they may not even scratch the surface of why they're here and how many times they've been here. Wow."

"We have now heard some very fascinating and potentially logical reasons why these UAPs might be coming here," Myrtle started, "and at this point world governments do not know the real reason for their visits, if in fact the five percent of UAP sightings, which we can't completely verify, mean anything other than all the possibilities raised here in the last few minutes."

"And now I suggest that we go out on the deck and reflect on all we've discussed and enjoy some snacks I made late last night."

Back from Snacks

"So far we've heard stories from all over the world, as well as in our oceans, but nothing from here in Massachusetts." Stuart paused. "There actually was a sighting right here in Boston!" He lifted his arm, then sharply lowered it with an emphatic "Yes!"

"It was at least four objects flying in a V-shaped formation. The sighting was at an air station, and a photograph was taken outdoors looking up at 9:35 a.m. on July 16, 1952.

"I'd like to share a few more examples, and then let's look at Grammy's chart and then Kate's and Myrtle's if that's okay with all of you." Stuart paused.

"It's okay with me," Grammy said.

"Ditto for Kate and me," Myrtle said.

"Great," came Stuart's reply. "Great!"

"What all my readings so far infer is that there have been UAP sightings around the world, yet a 2024 government report claimed that there is no—and I stress the word 'no'—absolute proof that UAPs are real. And yet, the 2004 Tic Tac sighting has a video showing an oblong object and validates that the object not only disappeared but was also sighted a minute later sixty miles away. I'd like to play that video now, and I'd like you to come closer to my computer."

Stuart then typed in *https://www.history.com/videos/uss-nimitz-tic-toc-ufo-declassified-video*, and up came the video.

"Well, after seeing that, what's your take on the government saying there's no proof, and yet here we see—and I'll finger-quote this—proof!"

"I tend to think in rather concrete terms," said Grammy, "and I feel the government wants an actual UAP on the ground that can be studied. Let me end by just saying that sightings, recorded or not, do not allow the US government to state that UAPs are real."

"I'm leaning in Grammy's direction regarding the premise of her statement just now. Kate and I have read quite a bit about UAPs, but again, to Grammy's point and the position of the US government, we don't have an actual UAP we can study. Plus, the speeds the sightings were able to go, as well as the G-forces implied, make it hard to confirm that UAPs are real. And with that I yield my seat."

Kate looked at her mom and said, "Oh, no, you're sounding like Stuart."

"Whaaat," came Stuart's loudly indignant voice. "On such a serious subject I'd never chuckle, although I did have fun with the Tic Tac candy." And then he smirked a wicked smile.

"Grammy is going to present next, but before she does, I have some more things to share from all my readings done so far. I know you want to hear Grammy's presentation, but these things I want to share will further enhance the power of the details she will be presenting.

"I've learned a great deal, seen certain patterns emerging in terms of the many encounters recorded to date, especially encounters with planes of different types.

"One pattern is the closeness of the UAPs to planes, and by that, I mean as close as thirty feet! That would be very scary for pilots! That's a near miss!" He paused.

"Reasons for a crash not happening could be attributed to the very high degree of maneuverability of the UAPs.

"Also, a factor was how a pilot would quickly shut down all the electronics which are basically flying the plane, and then take over the flying of the plane manually, with no technology being used as it was often corrupted by the UAPs. The plane's technology was made useless by the UAP.

"And in many cases, ground-based technology such as radar often did not detect the UAPs even though the UAPs were sighted by some of the people on board!"

"And now Grammy, you're on!"

"Stuart, I need you to go with me to the car to get something for my presentation. It's too heavy for me to carry."

The two of them left.

A minute later Grammy opened both doors so Stuart could walk in. He was carrying something of an awkward shape and weight.

"What's that?" Kate asked.

"It's an overhead projector. I just can't get used to using a computer to do such a presentation, so I asked Lauretta Kaye at the Oceanographic Institute to make overhead slides for me. I know, it's strange to be talking about UAPs in the modern era when I'm using old technology! And here I go!" And with that she turned on the overhead projector, put her slide on it, and focused the overhead.

"I chose these sightings to show you how some of the sightings have very different ranges presented because people see things differently and recall with less or more detail. After you study it, we'll discuss it."

Date	Location	# Seen	Describe Shape	Speed
7/8/47	Mojave Desert	1	Oval shape with two fins or nobs	rapid
1/7/48	Kentucky, Ohio, Rifer	1	250 feet-300 feet	average
3/24/67	Air Force Base, Montana	1	Glowing red oval; shut down 10 nuclear missiles	rapid
3/13/1997 6:55 p.m.	Henderson, Nevada	Hard to say	1 mile long; as wide as 2 football fields	Took off in a blink of an eye!
3/13/1997 8:15 p.m.	Arizona	Possibly several	Massive V-shaped or triangular in shape	Slow
1997, no month	Heading to Boston	1	Round with brilliant lights	?
Summer 1981	Over Lake Michigan	1	Size of a grapefruit, round; silver	1,000 mph
10/23/2002	North of Mobile, AL	1	Crashed into a plane; object not seen but a strange red residue on plane	?

# OF TURNS	Hovered	ON LAND	IN/ON SEA	IN AIR
				Yes
				Yes
	YES			Yes
0	Moved slowly			Yes
0				Yes
0				Yes
1	Very short Time			Yes
0				Yes

"My research found that in many cases the number of turns was not stated, and only the 'Hovered' column and the 'Air' column could be filled in. Any questions for me?"

"In your other research Grammy—and this chart is very good—did you encounter other discrepancies made by observers?" Myrtle asked.

"Yes, I did, but for the most part there was some

agreement, especially in the last five columns. Given that there are no more questions, let me ask this question: Do the column headings work for you?"

Stuart replied, "They work for me Grammy; just the differences in the fourth column tell me that we're going to see a lot of differences of opinion even on the same UAP sightings."

"I have a few quick things to share, but before I do, any more questions?" Grammy paused.

"Okay, just a few quick bits of insight I've gained," Grammy said, "and I'll start with a large book I looked at. It's written by Cheryl and Linda Costa. It contained just the basics of UAP sightings, and they used the term UFOs not UAPs as the book was assembled before 2024. The book contained very interesting charts and graphs for each state, and the charts and graphs cover a period from 2001 to 2015. Summer is the most frequent time that UAPs are seen, and the most frequent shapes sighted were lights, circles, and spheres." Grammy paused, looked at the group, and said, "Any more to ask?"

And with that Myrtle stood up and suggested, "Why don't we all go in the kitchen for a light supper?"

Everyone said, "Yes!" and headed for the kitchen.

After Dinner
a Few Brief Presentations
and then "Good Nights"

"Kate and Myrtle will now present their findings," Stuart softly said, "and then we'll conclude this meeting. At our next meeting," he turned to Masaneka, "we'll start with your presentation. And I must say what you," he looked at the other four, "are researching and sharing has been phenomenal. All of it will help me with my final report, and my boss has already complimented me for having the four of you on my team to expand the breadth and depth of the report, and most importantly, the opinion-related statements which cast a different slant on the overall study. So, thank you!

"And now, after a most enjoyable supper, I hand

the meeting over to Kate and Myrtle." Stuart then sat down next to Grammy.

Kate started. "The phrase 'saucer' was used by a man named Kenneth Arnold after a UAP sighting he made on June 24,1947 in Washington State. He was flying his plane when he saw a bright light and then realized he was looking at nine objects with hundred-foot diameter circular wingspans, all in formation, and moving at tremendous speed. He saw no external wings or the like for directional changes and no exhaust trail behind them.

"When Arnold shared his encounter with the press, he used the phrase 'saucer-shaped' to describe what he saw, and that's where the term 'flying saucer' originated!

"And a consistency in the sightings we've studied is the sighted UAPs have no external wings or the like for directional changes, as well as no exhaust trails, and they move in physics-defying maneuvers."

Kate then turned to Grammy. "Grammy, this is another sighting you can add to your chart."

"Thanks Kate, and I'd already written it down."

"Great, and from this point on as we do our detailed research, we'll share with you the necessary descriptors for your graph."

Grammy nodded in return.

"On June 28, 1947," Kate continued, "at 3:15 p.m., near Lake Mead, Nevada, six circular objects were reported by an F-51 Mustang pilot. That same night in Alabama," her voice went up at the last word, "a bright light was reported overhead before it made a ninety-degree turn and headed south.

"On July 4, four disk-shaped sightings were reported as streaking rapidly across the sky near Redmond, Washington. And on that same day at 1:05 p.m., in Portland, Oregon a police officer shared that he saw five large disks flying over the city, a sighting supported by two other police officers who saw the same thing!" Kate paused.

"On that same day, July 4, at 8:00 p.m. a flight going from Boise, Idaho to Oregon sighted somewhere between four and nine oval or saucer-like objects. So, as you can see, a lot happened that day!

"And I'll now close on this part of our report to reinforce that we've seen several examples during our readings of multiple sightings on the same day but at great distances from each other.

"Any questions before my mother takes over?"

"Wow," Masaneka said. "King told me of no sightings in the air, but instead, many in the waters around Saint Michael's and the islands which make up the Azores. He thought all the sightings by him and his people were just plates made by governments on the lands of Earth." Masaneka paused. "He's going to be very surprised when he hears what I've learned today and what I'll be learning as we go ahead. Wow!"

Kate smiled and nodded back to Masaneka.

"And now my mother will share about a major sighting called 'Phoenix Lights,' something Grammy showed you on her chart. Mom will share a great deal of details on that event, one that has been considered one of the biggest yet!"

Kate then sat down as Myrtle got up and began.

She looked at Masaneka and said, "I can't wait to hear what King will be telling you.

"And now, my presentation. The first thing I'm going to address is what's called 'Phoenix Lights' which happened in 1997 on March 13, around 8:00 p.m. to 8:15 p.m. Some of the facts are astounding. Hundreds, if not thousands of witnesses saw it! What's interesting is that some said they saw a triangular shape and others saw V shapes, and others saw a rectangular shape. Regardless, what was sighted was massive. The UAP came from the local mountain range, and besides the number of people who saw it, a film of this sighting was made. This filming was significant not only because it was the first sighting captured visually, but because it convinced many people that the government explanation was not, and I stress, *not,* the truth, especially for those who saw it themselves.

"It was hard to believe the government when they tried to refute it. What the people saw was a silently navigating UAP gliding above them. It was a sight no one had ever seen. It blocked the night sky and the stars from view. It was so low that people could make out details on the bottom side, which some felt was close enough to throw a stone at!

"This same object had been seen earlier at 6:53 p.m. in Henderson, Nevada. And we saw that on Grammy's overhead slide. One description of the Nevada sighting stated that it was the size of many football fields! Others described it as being as much as a mile long! It was described as gray in color, and it was eerily silent. Its lights and their colors were hard details to pin down. Some felt it was more than one craft. In the end, it sped away!

"Any questions for me?"

No one raised a question, and so Stuart took over.

"Tomorrow let's meet again around four. Okay?"

Everyone nodded.

"And Masaneka, you'll start off the meeting after my brief introduction. Okay?"

"Sounds like a plan, Stuart!"

Everybody chuckled at Masaneka's reply.

"And again Myrtle, thank you for sharing your delicious dinner!"

Everybody said, "Yes!" in unison!

4:00 p.m. at Myrtle and Kate's

Everyone was making small talk when Stuart stood up and suggested they start the meeting. Everyone nodded in agreement.

"Masaneka is on first, and then I have a fantastic proposal to make after my presentation! Yes!" Stuart ended with a sharp shaking of his right arm. "You're on Masaneka."

She stood up, scanned her notes, and began. "King and I spoke for about ten minutes, and although that was a short time, he covered everything. Then we just visited by using our laptops. And yes, King is now learning to use his computer, and he loves the games he can play. He is blown away by all the wonderful things available to him on the surface.

"But enough of that. What he shared with me is

not too different from what I've shared before with the exception of a few details.

"Picking up on previous sightings I've shared, King said that many such sightings have been seen by the people of Atlantis for many generations. The most common theme was much like the one where we would see one or two or even many more UAPs resting against the under-ocean part of Saint Michael's. There was only one time that over two hundred were seen. We've also never seen anything other than flying saucers.

"But then he went looking for stories from several of our colonies on the edges of the Atlantic Ocean. Two of the colonies shared that they had seen what seemed to be a resting place for saucers. Sometimes the saucers would stay in formation, and there seemed to be one large saucer that never flew up to the surface. The slightly smaller saucers would pull right up to the larger one and somehow connect to it. I can only compare it to an airport and that thing we walk on to get to the plane or leave the plane, but their smaller saucer just connected directly to the larger saucer."

"Excuse me Masaneka," Stuart said, "but there were several other saucers which did the same thing as to connecting to the larger saucer, right?"

"Yes, that's how it was described."

"Wow!" Stuart said. "Wait till you hear what I'll be sharing. What you just shared might prove a theory the government has about such a sight. Wow." Stuart sat down.

"Should I continue?" she asked.

"Yes, of course," Stuart replied.

"Only one other such site was ever seen, and that was off the coast of Newfoundland. It was described as easily three times the size of the one I just spoke about. I say three times the size as there were three larger saucers that seemed to stay in the same place while others came to them, hooked up somehow, and then backed away a short time later. The colonists never went close to these sites for fear that they might kill us if they saw us."

Looking at Stuart she said, "You have shared sightings of very different shaped saucers such as the Tic Tac shape. My people have not seen anything other than the saucers which we call plates. We also never saw the round shape inside a square." She paused. "Or was it a square inside a round sphere?'

"I've forgotten which way it is," Stuart laughed.

He then continued, "That was some series of observations your people saw, and the last one is of a theory the US government and other governments have, and that is the UAPs have sites in our oceans which compare to the airports we have on land.

Wow!" He shook his head and said nothing for a few seconds.

Everyone else did much the same.

Mrytle then spoke, saying in a soft and questioning tone of voice, "These sightings by the Atlanteans are quite frightening. It's also conclusive proof that the saucers have an underwater airport, or should I say seaport?" She put her hand to her mouth and just stared.

"Anything else Masaneka?" Stuart asked.

"Nothing more than that, except to remind you of the one interaction with one of the plates, I mean saucers," she said with a chuckle, "that two of our teenagers had when they tapped the saucer, and it opened, and when the two teenagers offered the gold coins."

"Thank you Masaneka. What you just shared has profound implications for all the governments." He went silent, just thinking. Then he looked up at the other four in the room and said, "I'll share now what I've researched."

He took a sip of water and began. "Satellites and AI are now being put into use to monitor potential UAP occurrences not only here in the USA, but in other countries. What Masaneka just shared supports that this use of satellites and AI must continue." He paused. "Wow!

"This use of technology is also being implemented off the coast of California because of so many sightings in this part of the world. The goal is to find scientific evidence as to whether UAPs are *real*!

"I now have a big surprise to share! My boss has suggested I go to Catalina Island within the next few days! Are you at all able to make such plans with such short notice?"

Grammy spoke first. "I'm all for it as it's just me I must worry about. But we should all plan to be on the same plane, okay?"

"Absolutely Grammy," Myrtle said, "and all I have to do is get Dr. Fuller to give me the okay to go." And then she turned to Kate and Masaneka. "Are you two ready to go?"

The two girls looked at each other, nodded their heads, and said, "Yes!" with lots of enthusiasm in their voices.

"Well, I guess it's settled. I'll have the boss's secretary find the first flight we can take, let's say, two days from today if that's alright with the four of you. She'll call each of you for details and for charge numbers."

They all yelled in unison, "Yes!"

"Great. I'll speak to her first thing tomorrow morning. But now I want to share what I've learned about UAP sightings in, on, and over the Pacific, sightings that the people of Catalina have experienced.

"The first thing I encountered was the word wormhole. It's basically a long, tubular tunnel with one end in some place in space and the other end at a place here on Earth, and in this case, it either ends in the space above Catalina Island, or in the ocean near the island. Travel through such a wormhole would allow a saucer to cut out billions of miles of travel and the time it would take, allowing the saucer to travel long distances in very short times. Another word used is a portal, which means the same as a wormhole.

"There was one early morning sighting of a black wormhole, observed in the sky just before dawn. Physicists saw it, and within the black hole they saw what looked like small bright lights which they assumed to be saucers about to arrive on Earth!

"The physicists and scientists realized that they had a real mystery in all this. They realized that UAPs could easily enter some place on Earth, and in this case, it was Catalina Island. Such a gateway to the island gives UAPs easy access to any place on Earth!"

Stuart paused, took a sip, and contemplated the

implications of what he just shared with Grammy, Myrtle, Kate, and Masaneka.

No one spoke a word. They just thought on what he had just shared as well.

"Okay, folks, I'm ready to continue on a slightly different tack, if I might use such a nautical term. This involves another acronym, USOs, or 'unidentified submersible objects.' Many experienced scientists, military personnel of all branches of our military, and even regular people have suspected that USOs existed off the coast of Catalina Island. Strange lights, softly lighted clouds in the ocean, and UAPs flying in and out of the oceans. And such occurrences happened in the nighttime.

"This is what has led to the possibility of UAP airports deep under the ocean!"

He then turned to Masaneka and said, "This is the phenomenon that the people of Atlantis observed, and it's what you just shared. Wow! Wow! Wow!" Stuart ended this part of his speech and took another sip of water.

"And to think that the Atlanteans thought it was just you people on Earth!" Masaneka said in a soft and muted voice.

"Yes, Masaneka, the Atlanteans saw such things before leading scientists and military knew what they were looking at. And your people shared only sightings in the Atlantic, not in the Pacific!"

"That is correct as our people never went to the Pacific. I did not know that there were so many other huge bodies of water such as the Pacific, the Indian Ocean, and even the Great Lakes!"

"Yes, Masaneka, seventy percent of Earth is covered in water, but what you shared a few minutes ago validates much of what is now being stated as real, such as an underwater UAP sighting off the southern California coast. That area, which is also near Catalina Island, has had sightings they are starting to share. Over the last thirty years they've seen UAPs cruising on the ocean, spheres of different shapes as well as colors of light in flight, cloud-like cigars huge in size, and," Stuart paused, "you'll get a kick out of this one: a UAP sighting when the aliens were in uniform!

"And that's all I have to share! Let's go to Catalina!"

Catalina Island

After their arrival in Los Angeles Airport, they went by van to Long Beach, California, and from there they took a boat ride to Avalon, the harbor city of Catalina.

"So far so good, Stuart," Grammy said as she looked at Stuart, and then at how far from Long Beach and the mainland of California they'd be. "What do you think will be next?"

"Don't know Grammy, don't know." Stuart seemed anxious and yet deep in thought.

Masaneka turned to Myrtle. "Is the Pacific always this calm?"

"Basically, yes," Myrtle replied. "Think of the word pacific spelled with a lowercase P." She paused. "The word 'pacific' means peaceful or tranquil, and the Pacific Ocean has far less waves than what you are used to in the Atlantic Ocean. Does that help?"

"Interesting," Masaneka replied. "That makes sense."

The five of them watched as the coast of California got smaller and smaller until you could only see the tops of tall buildings. Then Grammy yelled out, "There's Catalina!"

Everyone looked.

"It's getting close to evening, so let's hope we get to see some of the island," Stuart stated. "Want to see the buffalo ranch?"

"There are buffalo on Catalina?" Kate asked in surprise.

"Yes, a small herd. The original owners of the island were the Wrigleys, the makers of the gum, and I think that they brought them here when they owned the entire island! Imagine that!"

"This place is already getting interesting and we're not even there yet," Kate said.

"And I don't know about the four of you, but I'm hungry," Myrtle said. "I'd like to suggest that we get settled in our rooms and then go to a good place for dinner. After we can walk around Avalon and get our boat ride tickets for tomorrow. That sound okay?" Myrtle proposed.

"Sounds good," was everyone's answer.

"Avalon looks like a cute town as we start getting closer to it," Kate said. "But the buffalo thing really has me wondering why Mr. Wrigley brought them here."

"Who knows," Stuart said as he shrugged his shoulders. "Who knows."

The boat captain then spoke. "Please sit down until after we tie up at the dock. It's high tide tonight, so you'll have an easy walk up the plank to the dock. Just keep in mind that there will be a small amount of rocking caused by the small waves."

Everyone sat.

"Oh, look," Grammy said, "I can see our hotel, and it's only two blocks away."

Everyone looked.

"The boat is tied up to the dock, so please proceed with caution, and have a wonderful stay," the captain stated in a strong voice.

In no time they were on land and heading to the hotel.

"After each of us checks in and cleans up a bit, we can meet in the lobby at seven, okay?" Myrtle asked.

Everyone agreed.

They all sighed and went to their rooms. Kate and Masaneka shared a room.

Around seven everyone was in the lobby.

"I just asked the hotel clerk for a good place to

eat, and he said to just go next door as they have a good menu," Myrtle said. "So let's eat!"

And next door they went.

After a good meal they went for a short walk as it was getting darker.

"I'm pretty pooped, and by East Coast time it's now half past midnight," Grammy said. "I think I'm going to bed, but before I do, what time is our tour boat?"

"It's at nine forty-five, just down the wharf from where we landed," said Stuart. "And going to bed is where I'm heading as dinner was good!"

Everyone laughed, and they all headed to the hotel and their rooms.

The Boat Ride Along the Coast of Catalina

"All aboard," came a voice from the boat tied to the wharf.

"It's showtime!" Stuart yelped out.

Everyone laughed, and then they boarded the boat.

"My name is Ella, and I'll be your guide today. We'll go up the coast of Catalina to the northeastern-most point, and then we'll turn back. The San Pedro Channel which separates us from the mainland is nice and calm today, so we'll have a smooth ride. I'll point out many sights along the way, and at noon I'll be serving sandwiches, coffee, and soda." Ella paused and then asked, "Any questions for me?"

Stuart immediately raised his hand and said, "I have a couple."

"Great! Please ask them," replied Ella.

"Will you be pointing out any locations where there were UAP sightings?"

"I sure will," Ella replied. "I'll also point out where here in the channel there have been under-channel sightings. How does that sound?"

"Great!"

"Then let's push off Captain."

Ella began her presentation after leaving the harbor in Avalon. "The San Pedro Channel has been a major source of underwater sightings. One of the suspicions is that there may be a UAP underwater base in the channel. Sightings have been made of UAPs going into and out of the channel, and most of them have been in the early hours of the morning, in the four a.m. time frame, just before people start waking and/or driving to work. We've also experienced several instances of lights fifty to one hundred feet below the surface."

Kate whispered to Stuart, "Is this what you wanted?"

"Yes, and then some. Wow!"

After a few minutes Ella spoke again. "One of the strangest sightings was in about this area off the coast of the island. It was out maybe about two miles." She pointed away from the island. "An underwater UAP was sighted well below the surface, but inside the UAP occupants were visible and in uniforms!

"For quite some time now neighbors on the mainland and visitors here on the island have gone to the shore in the evening in hopes of catching a sight of the various colored UAPs which now and then would appear and sink into the Channel. Those are one of the sources of lights we've seen in the Channel. You'll have to look this evening."

About ten minutes passed.

"Stuart," Myrtle whispered to him, "will this help with your research?"

"It sure will! And I'm going to walk along the beach tonight in hopes of seeing something."

Ella spoke again. "We're now about twenty-five miles from Avalon. What I'd like to point out now is that the area on that part of the island is where the herd of buffalo can be found. You can get to them from Avalon by renting a golf cart and going out to where they graze. The area is fenced off so it's safe, and don't try to feed them as they might get sick from it." Ella then sat down.

After about five minutes Ella stood up and said, "Please look east now towards the mainland. It is in this area where the most actual sightings have been made of UAPs rising out of the channel. What's strange is that the observations have been consistent as to what witnesses have seen and heard!" Ella paused after dramatically raising her voice. "And what they've seen has not only been saucer-shaped UAPs but also UAPs just floating along the surface of the channel. What's interesting is that there was no visible source of propulsion or exhaust. How they're able to do it is a great mystery."

"This is blowing my mind Stuart," Masaneka said. "It's just like what we saw below Saint Michael's."

"It's blowing my mind, too, Masaneka. What's she going to share next?"

As if on cue, Ella spoke. "It's now eleven fifteen, so I'm going to go around with the sandwich cart. Take a sandwich, and there are a variety of them, as well as a beverage or a coffee." Ella pushed the cart around to the twenty or so people on the boat and people took out what they wanted for lunch.

Grammy spoke before biting into her sandwich. "This has been a most pleasant time so far. The scenery is beautiful and the UAP episodes are sure spooky. I'm glad I came Stuart, as now I really realize the size and scope of the UAP concerns."

"I couldn't agree with you more Grammy. I'm loving it." Stuart took a bite of his sandwich.

"Yes, Stuart, what Grammy said is so true, and to be where this stuff has happened makes it even more anxiety provoking. Phew!" Myrtle said.

"I'm just pleased to now know that the size and areas covered by these UAPs is basically the entire world. In the Atlantic we thought that they were done by you surface people in a new kind of boat!" Masaneka chuckled.

Kate had just begun to speak when Ella started up again. "Northeast from here in the direction of Santa Monica beach, a man named Frederick Hehr sighted a squadron of saucers doing maneuvers over the bay," and then she added, "and by over the bay I mean in *the sky*!" Ella paused to let it sink in. "They did the same thing later in the day for about ten minutes." Then she sat down and looked at all the passengers, who were doing what all the passengers she had did after that announcement. That is, just staring out at the water with a shocked look on their faces and their jaws dropped open.

She began again. "One story is about three men on the mainland who saw the UAP occupants! They walked up to the three men and tried to speak to them, but it was in a language the men could not understand. The saucer occupants then returned to their UAP and were gone in a flash!

"Back in the seventies a man sailing his boat witnessed a metallic saucer with four pods underneath it, flying a couple hundred feet above water.

"A little later in the seventies, a man saw a

metallic saucer with a metallic dome on its top and bottom, and it looked like two plates put together."

"What?" came Masaneka's unusually loud voice. "Did you say plates?"

"Yes, but why do you ask so loudly?"

"This will surprise you and the other passengers on the boat, but I came from the colony of Atlantis under Saint Michael's in the Azores, and in Atlantis we called them plates, not saucers."

"What? You're from Atlantis?" Ella was stunned. "I've read about your coming out of the ocean to live on the land in the country of Portugal. Right?"

"Yes."

Everyone was looking in a most stunned way at Masaneka.

One woman passenger asked, "You mean that was real, the thing about Atlantis?"

"Yes, it was," Masaneka replied. "The pollution of the oceans had gotten so bad that we could no longer live in secrecy under Saint Michael's. Our babies were dying. And I was the last child of Atlantis. Now our people are having children again but are living now and forever on the land."

"Wow!" another passenger said. "This trip just went over the top for mind-boggling things that have and are now happening! Wow!"

Ella stood up to regain control of the audience.

"This is surely a most wonderful thing to have happened young lady. What is your name?"

"My name is Masaneka, and I am the granddaughter of the king of Atlantis, and I am a princess."

"This is a trip I'll never forget," Ella said softly, shaking her head. "But now on a signal from the captain we have reached the northern tip of Catalina, and we must now turn back. I have more observations to share, but they sure will pale in compassion to what you just shared young lady."

Masaneka smiled back with a nod.

Stuart reached over and patted her on the back. "Well done, Masaneka, well done."

"Thanks Stuart. It's just that I thought it was funny to hear Ella describe the UAPs as plates."

"This trip just keeps getting better!" Kate said with her voice rising.

Grammy and Myrtle looked at each other, hugged, and then smiled.

"We're turning now," Ella said, "and on the way back I'll share some more actual UAP happenings. UAPs have been seen along the coast in very large numbers, and they're usually flying about two thousand feet or so above the water. This entire channel area is a hotbed for UAP sightings as you can tell by the first half of the trip. Sightings have been made on the island, but very few when compared to channel sightings. I've been told that people have had strange experiences on the island, but I have no proof of such occurrences.

"What we do know is that these UAPs frequently fly in and out of the channel waters as well as the Pacific side of Catalina. We're referred to as a hot spot for UAP sightings!" Ella sat down and sipped her coffee.

"What do you think of this so far Stuart?" Grammy asked.

"I feel like I'm in a strange place. I don't even feel like I'm on the boat with all of you. I just feel strange."

Myrtle looked at him, and thought to herself, 'Leave well enough alone.'

Ella, putting her coffee cup down, got up to initiate the next phase of the tour. "I'm going to share a few more stories as we go along, and after each story I'll take a break so you can enjoy the view. We should be back in Avalon about one o'clock." She paused and checked with the captain who gave her a nod in agreement.

"What was at first thought to be a submarine was later thought to be a UAP. South of Catalina by about six miles the captain of a chartered fishing boat saw what was at first thought to be a submarine with five men in varying attire on the top of the sub as it was slowly floating on the surface. As the fishing boat got closer the supposed sub increased its speed and headed towards the fishing boat. The captain made a quick change in direction, and what was first believed to be a sub was later felt to be a UAP. It passed the fishing boat with no sound, no exhaust, and no wake. It's one of those sightings that was never fully agreed upon."

A good ten minutes passed before Ella began again. "The next incident I'll share happened off the southern end of the island. A man fishing from his boat spotted a white dome-shaped object. He saw the object rise about ten feet off the surface and then descend and ascend again. It had some kind of strange cloth object under it that seemed to be moving up and down in the water. This was also suspected to be a UAP, but what was it doing? Was it getting samples from the water? Was it experimenting? What was it doing? These types of observations are not unusual in this area, and we do not always know what they are here for." With that Ella sat down.

Stuart turned to Kate and said, "This is so beautiful and yet so bizarre when you hear what Ella is sharing. When we return, I'm going to ask her if she has any hard copy references that I can bring back with me or have mailed. What's your take so far?"

Masaneka scooted over and sat close to Kate. "Well, I believe that she's telling the truth, and the reputation of this island supports her stories, but I'm more perplexed now than I ever was. I mean, this stuff is really sounding like there really are UAPs in these waters and in this area of California."

"I agree!" Masaneka said. "What's different for me is how varied the descriptions are of the UAPs compared to the saucers we saw in the waters off Saint Michael's. Also, what surprises me is how many years the people of California have seen the UAPs."

"Yup, this is conclusive proof that UAPs are real. If only we had some kind of absolute proof."

"If anyone would like another sandwich, there are some left. Beverages as well," Ella added.

Everyone just sat back and enjoyed the cruise and did a lot of pondering about what all this could mean.

Fifteen minutes later Ella spoke again. "The next stories are about colored lights. In the early nineties there were several sightings of colorful lights in the water. In one of them, a fireball-like object descended from the sky at a rather rapid rate and then disappeared into the water. One sighting was glowing disks while the other was one light going back and forth about a hundred feet above the water while two other lights were moving back and forth under the water.

"There are many other stories I could have told you, but this boat trip is about enjoying the ride and the scenery as well as hearing true observations made by citizens and our military. I'm going to finish with why authorities feel that there are so many sightings in this area of Catalina Island.

"The suspicion is that there's a UAP underwater base. It is believed that people have been abducted and brought there for observations and tests. These are a mix of suspicious happenings as well as real happenings. People have said they were abducted, studied, and returned, but when they 'returned' their stories sounded more like dreams than not. Many of the stories implied the existence of an underwater landing base where they were taken. Others who have not experienced an abduction feel strongly about a landing base because of all the UAP sightings in this part of California. One abductee described the examiners as praying mantis type in appearance. Yuck!"

Ella sat down.

Stuart, Kate, and Masaneka chatted about all Ella had shared while Myrtle and Grammy just sat back and enjoyed the ride.

A short time later Ella spoke again. "We're

almost back to the harbor in Avalon, so please check to be sure all your belongings are together. This has been a very different experience given that we have a princess of Atlantis with us." Ella nodded at Masaneka.

"Thank you," Masaneka said back.

"As you leave the boat, we're at mid-tide so you'll have to walk carefully up the plank. Use the railing if you need it. Thank you all and have a wonderful afternoon and evening." Ella then quickly jumped on the wharf and tied up the boat. Then she lowered the gangplank and waved the passengers off the boat.

*A Walk Down to the Buffalo Ranch
and Then to Bed!*

"When we get to the hotel, let's meet in the lobby and figure out what we want to do for the rest of the day, okay?" Myrtle said.

"I'm for that," Grammy said, "and I'm sure happy that the channel was so calm. And I'm just in awe of all the stories Ella told us. I mean, I've done the charts, heard from you all, and yet I'm still uncertain about UAPs."

"You've got my vote on that one Grammy," Kate offered.

"Mine, too." said Myrtle. "What about you Stuart and you Masaneka?"

"I believe they exist," said Masaneka. "I mean, I've seen them, my fellow Atlanteans have seen them, and Ella's stories today were just too real to deny."

"And I'm on the same page as Masaneka, and today's boat ride and some of my research on the channel and on Catalina tell me it's for real." Then Stuart leaned back on the sofa and raised his arms up with a shrug. "What I don't get is why they are here."

Kate finished by saying, "I'm leaning more to Stuart's side, but what he just said is what's holding me up and that is, why, why are they here?"

"Heavy stuff my good friends, very heavy stuff. But may I now suggest that we go to our rooms, clean up, and come back in an hour. I'd like to eat at the same place as last time, and after go to the buffalo ranch. What do you think?" Myrtle said, holding her hands up in question. "All in favor say yes, and those against say no!"

The other four answered in unison: "Yes!"

With that they headed to their respective rooms, and then an hour later they gradually gathered all together and headed to the restaurant!

"Well, another good meal! So, what's next?" Grammy said as she wiped her lips. "How do we get to the buffalo farm?"

Kate quickly answered, "We can go in two golf carts, but we must be sure to tell them to come back at a certain time to pick us up. How long do you think we'll be there?"

"I talked to the front desk at the hotel," Stuart said, "and the lady said that an hour is enough time to spend there, and that it takes about fifteen minutes to get there. So, let's let them know that they should come and get us an hour after they drop us off. Okay?"

"Sounds good. Let's go find two golf carts!" Kate jovially yelled out.

"Uh, they're right next to the hotel?" Stuart said in a condescending voice. "See?" he pointed.

Kate spats back, "Oh, Stuart, you are our savior." And she gave him a high five.

Masaneka just looked on and shook her head, but she also had a big smile!

In no time they arrived at the entrance to the buffalo farm. It was a huge place, and the buffalo were visible way on the other side of the pasture.

A man in jeans and high boots greeted them. "Welcome to the buffalo farm. You may walk around the fences, and that will take you a good mile down. You can then take the woodland trail around the fenced in area for a short distance of about a third of a mile before the trail stops. Then turn around and head back. That'll take about fifty minutes roundtrip. And do not, and I stress *do not* go any further than the end of the woodland trail. Any questions?"

"Why such stern words about not going any further in the woodland trail?" Stuart asked.

"It's very simple. Supposedly there's a vortex in that area, and several people who have gone beyond the end of the path have had strange experiences and very long-lasting fatigue. Does that answer your question?"

"Yes, and thank you," Stuart replied.

"Let's get going," Grammy said, "but I'm only going to walk halfway down the fence, and then I'm going to walk back and wait. That's too long a walk for me."

"Okay Grammy," Myrtle said, and then she turned to the four kids and said, "Let's go!"

Off they went.

At the halfway point Grammy said, "This is it for me. I'm going to head back and wait. This has been just beautiful, but I don't want to get sore from a long walk."

"We should be back in about forty minutes Grammy, so enjoy your rest, and when we get back, I want to go right back to the hotel and go to sleep!" Kate said.

"Me, too," Masaneka.

"And I'll second the motion!" Myrtle chuckled out, and off they all went.

When they got to the beginning of the woodland trail, they stopped.

"I can't wait to walk into this jungle-like path," Stuart chimed out. "Yes!"

"Mom, I'm pooped. And I think I'd like to go back," Kate said in a tired voice.

"I'm for that, too," Masaneka said in a soft voice. "This is probably the longest walk I've ever taken!"

"The longest?" Stuart asked.

"Yes, as even in high school I take a bus, so I'm not in shape for this walking stuff! I'd much rather be swimming!"

"Okay, Kate and Masaneka, head back, and," Myrtle turned to Stuart, "I'll wait here for you, and then we can head back together. Okay?"

"Sure, Myrtle. I just want to see if I experience the vortex."

With that Stuart started on the path and Kate and Masaneka headed back to the barn area to sit with Grammy. Myrtle stood for a few minutes until Stuart was out of sight. Then she turned and looked out across the stretch of land, enjoying the very different plants and flowers.

Ten minutes later she looked at her watch and wondered what was holding Stuart up.

"Stuart," she called out in a strong voice. But no reply. "Stuart," she yelled out again. Silence.

"Rats," she murmured. "I guess I have to go on the path and into the woods." And then she mumbled to herself, "I hope that vortex thing isn't for real." And off she went.

Five minutes later she yelled for Stuart again and she got no answer. "Where is he?" she questioned in a soft voice.

Then suddenly she saw a large branch of big leaves move. She froze.

And out came Stuart, looking very strange.

"Stuart," Myrtle softly asked, "are you okay?"

He looked up at her with a puzzled stare. He just stood there, his face had a vacant look, and his shoulders were slouched very visibly. "I found," and he paused, "the vortex. But something else was there."

"What else was there?" she asked.

"I don't know. I just began to feel this strange sense that my muscles were going soft, and I just flopped down on a log. I couldn't move until I heard you yell for me. I still feel strange. I'm scared."

"I'm sure you'll be okay. Let's walk back." And with that she went over to where he was and gently took his hand.

"Ahhhh!" he yelped out, staring at Myrtle.

"What is it, Stuart?" Myrtle questioned.

He looked at her. "When did you get here?" he asked in a confused whisper.

"I've been here talking to you for a minute or two. Do you not remember me asking you if you were okay?"

He looked at her, dazed. "Should we go back to the barn?"

"Yes." And with that she slowly pulled his hand to get him to start walking.

"Let's start walking back Stuart. Okay?" she said in a very soft voice, still holding his hand.

He looked at her and then started walking slowly. They walked hand in hand to the end of the woodland path to the main path. "Walk ahead of me Stuart." She pushed their gripped hands forward, and then he began to walk.

After almost twenty minutes they got back to the barn and saw Grammy, Kate, and Masaneka looking at them at the beginning of the path.

"Is Stuart alright?" Grammy asked Myrtle.

"He's had a strange experience, and he's not really with us or has his usual energy right now," Myrtle replied.

"What do you mean?" Grammy asked, raising her hand to her chin.

"Let's get to the golf cart and head back. I'll

explain it back at the hotel. He just needs to sit and relax."

"Okay," Grammy said. "I'll sit next to him on the way back."

Puzzled, everyone walked to the two golf carts, got on, and in no time the carts headed back to the hotel.

At the hotel, Grammy got off her golf cart very carefully and said, "I'll walk him in. He didn't say a word all the way back." She lowered her head and gently shook it.

Everyone followed Grammy and Stuart as Grammy guided him into the hotel.

They all headed to the couches and sat down, silent.

Myrtle began. "He was late in coming back to the path, so I went onto the woodland path calling for him. The first time he didn't reply. The second time he came from behind a large branch and just stared at me. I spoke to him, and he replied. But a few seconds later he had no recollection of replying. I continued speaking with him and he began to focus on me and spoke a few words. He said that he found a vortex and was caught up in it." She paused.

"Stuart," Masaneka said, "look at me."

Slowly he lifted his head up. "What?"

And suddenly Masaneka snapped her fingers very loudly in his face.

Everyone sat up in surprise, including Stuart.

"What's the matter?" he said. "Why did you do that?"

"I snapped my fingers to get you out of your trance, and it worked!"

She sat down.

Grammy asked him what he experienced in the vortex.

"All of a sudden, a swirl of air like a small cyclone surrounded me. I had a hard time breathing. Then suddenly it stopped. I looked down and at first, I couldn't figure out why there were two shadows beside me. When I turned around to see what was behind me the shadow disappeared. I felt weird. Then I heard a voice, and I thought it was Myrtle's. That's all I remember. And then on the golf cart ride back I started to figure out what was happening." He paused, and then he said, "I'd like to go to bed."

"A good idea," Grammy said.

Kate said, "Masaneka and I want to walk down to the wharf and watch the seagulls. Then we'll head back to the hotel. Okay?"

"Sure girls, sure, and just don't get caught in a vortex! And remember, we fly back tomorrow so pack up," Myrtle said.

"And be down here for a light breakfast by eight."

A Short Morning Before Heading to LA Airport

Myrtle was enjoying her coffee at the hotel's breakfast area when Grammy came over.

"That's just what I was dreaming about, a cup of coffee!"

The two of them chatted for a while.

Then the girls arrived.

"Donuts! Yeah!" Masaneka said. "I love them!"

"You're too funny about donuts!" Kate laughed.

Masaneka nodded her head in agreement but said nothing as her mouth was full.

"I wonder where the vortex boy is?" Grammy said. "I hope he slept well."

Twenty minutes passed.

"Masaneka and Kate, would you two mind going up and getting Stuart?" Mrytle said. "And make sure he's packed."

The girls left to check on Stuart, and Grammy and Myrtle just chatted about things.

Ten minutes later, the girls came down, very upset. "Mom, Stuart isn't answering the door."

"Oh, no," exclaimed Grammy. "I'll go up and wake him."

A few minutes later she was back and not with Stuart. "He didn't answer. What do I do?"

"Let's get the master key from the front desk and go up and open his door." With that all four of them went to the front desk, got a master key, and went to his room.

Grammy knocked again, softly, and uttered, "Stuart, it's Grammy. Wake up."

Nothing.

"Here's the master key Grammy." Myrtle handed it to her.

Grammy opened the door. She looked in slowly. She saw Stuart standing beside the bed with a white rag in his hand. "Stuart, you need to get dressed, get packed, and have breakfast."

He neither moved nor acknowledged his grandmother.

"Is something wrong Grammy?" Myrtle posed in a soft voice.

"It's as if he's in a trance. He's just standing there in his PJs with a rag in his hand."

"A rag? Why would he have a rag?"

"I don't know."

"Go over to him and take him by the hand and see if he'll move," Myrtle suggested while the two girls just listened from the corridor.

Grammy went over to Stuart and took his hand. "Come with me honey. You need breakfast." She pulled his hand. No movement. "Stuart, come with me now!" She was getting angry.

"I was in a flying saucer last night." He spoke softly. "They took me there. I never saw them. I walked around the inside of the saucer. I saw no one. I saw no equipment. All I got was this rag that was on the floor of the saucer." And he lifted the rag to show her.

"I don't know what to think Stuart, but you must get dressed, and you must pack your things as we leave in an hour. Get dressed and come down to the lobby for a light breakfast, *now*!" Frustration was making Grammy loud.

Grammy then took the rag from his hand and left his room, but as she got to the door of his room she said, "If you're not down in the lobby in fifteen minutes I'm going to come up and pull you out. Do you understand?"

"Yes."

Grammy came into the corridor, and the others were all standing there confused and concerned.

Grammy gave the rag to Myrtle and said, "This is not like any rag I've ever seen."

Myrtle looked at it. She rubbed it. She smelled it. She tried to tear it. She stretched it. "Nothing, Grammy, nothing," she said in a soft and confused tone of voice. "Nothing."

"May I see it?" Masaneka asked.

"Of course." Myrtle replied.

Masaneka opened it up and poured her OJ into it. It made a puddle, but it did not leak through. "Wow! The OJ didn't even stick to it, but made a pool." She turned to Myrtle. "Is it made of rubber or plastic?"

"I don't know Masaneka. So far it defies logic as to being a rag."

Then Stuart's door opened, and he stepped out, confused by everyone there. He just stared. "Why are you here, and why is there OJ in the rag? And how did you get ahold of it?"

"I'm sorry Stuart, but the rag defies logic. While we were waiting for you, we did some experiments. I'd like to keep it until I get back to the institute. What I'll do is more analysis of this rag."

Then Grammy looked at him, puzzled. "I was

just in your room Stuart, getting you to get ready. Don't you remember that?"

"No. But I thought we were supposed to be leaving soon."

Grammy looked at Myrtle with a confused and concerned startle.

"Well, we're all here, so let's get to the lobby and check out so we can get the boat back to the mainland, okay?" Myrtle asked in a puzzled tone of voice.

Stuart started walking to the elevator. His walk was like that of a robot, very deliberate and very even. Everyone stared. Then Myrtle waved to the others to follow him.

Not a word was spoken on the elevator.

When the elevator door opened, all got off but Stuart.

Grammy looked back at him. She walked to him. "Stuart, it's time to get off the elevator."

He looked at her and walked out. She followed.

Myrtle, Kate, and Masaneka just looked at the two of them, puzzled.

Grammy took his hand in hers and walked over to the hotel clerk and told Stuart to check out.

He looked at her. "What?"

"Check out."

He stared.

Grammy said, "Give me your wallet so I can get your charge card and sign you out."

He looked puzzled. Then he reached into his back pocket. "My wallet is not there."

"Is it in your room?" Grammy asked.

"I don't know."

"Do you have your room key Stuart?" Kate asked. "If not, I'll run up and look for it."

He felt his pockets. "I don't have it."

"I'll run up and look for it," Kate said, and off she went.

The others just stared at Stuart. He was not himself. He just stood there as if frozen.

Masaneka walked over to him and snapped her fingers near his face, and he jumped back and screamed.

"What are we standing here for?" he asked in an angry voice.

"We're checking out from the hotel, and since you forgot your room key, Kate ran up to get it. And here she comes now," Myrtle answered.

"Here's his key and his wallet, and his toiletries bag. You forgot everything Stu," Kate said in a most puzzled voice.

"Okay everyone, check out!" Myrtle said in a somewhat angry and puzzled voice.

Once checked out they headed for the wharf

and got on the boat which would take them back to Long Beach. From there they'd head to LA Airport, and head back to Woods Hole on Cape Cod.

On the plane back to Massachusetts, hardly anyone spoke. They'd look now and then at Stuart who was just sitting there like a statue, not moving a muscle.

"Do you think he really was on a UAP?" Grammy asked Myrtle.

"I'm beginning to think that he was, and the supposed rag defies all logic for a rag."

Stuart never moved, and when the stewardess offered him a light breakfast, he just looked at her, puzzled.

"He probably won't eat anything on the trip," Grammy said to herself.

Kate and Masaneka were across the aisle from him, and they weren't sure what to make of it.

Suddenly Stuart yelled out. "Stop touching me!"

"I'm sorry buddy, but I just want to get up to use the toilet. Please let me get by."

Stuart stared at him. Then Grammy got out of her seat and came over to him and whispered, "Just stand up so the man sitting next to you can go to the bathroom. And when he comes back, stand up so he can get to his seat."

Stuart looked at her, and then he got up to let the man out.

The man gave him a dirty look.

Stuart sat down.

Grammy waited, her hand on the back of his seat, waiting till the man came back.

When he returned, Grammy raised her hand to signal that she'd get him to stand up. She whispered gently in his ear to please get up so the man could get back to his seat.

Stuart did so, and the man sat back down. Then, so did Stuart.

Grammy took her seat as well.

The rest of the flight was fine, but Stuart just sat there staring.

Finally, they landed at Boston's Logan Airport. They got their luggage, keeping an eye on Stuart who had not come out of his extremely pensive state of mind, and headed to the main exit. There, waiting for them, was Stuart's company van.

They loaded up and off they went to Woods Hole on Cape Cod.

What's next?

The Rag!

"Good morning, Grammy. It's Myrtle, and I'm about to head to the institute to do some experiments on Stuart's rag. But I want to know how he's doing."

"He's still in a daze," Grammy whispered, "and so I'm driving him to his job. What he doesn't know is that I'm going to speak with his boss once Stuart's at his desk, and then let his boss know what might have happened and then describe his behavior. I'm hoping he'll send him home, so I'm going to wait and see if that happens."

"Sounds good Grammy. I'll check with you later, but while Masaneka is still here, I'm suggesting we think about the two of you coming to my place, possibly even at lunch time, that's if his boss sends him home, then that could be a good time for me to fill him in on my analysis of his rag. Would that work for you?"

"Yes, definitely. He just walked into the kitchen. I'll call you to let you know what his boss decides."

Myrtle headed to the institute.

Grammy and Stuart headed to his job.

At the institute, Myrtle and two of her colleagues studied and analyzed the rag. There was a great deal of confusion and questioning about what they'd discovered.

At eleven thirty, Myrtle called Grammy.

"Hi Grammy, it's me. How is Stuart doing?"

"Well, his boss agreed with me, and he told him to go to his grandmother's house and get some rest. He told Stuart that he had called his grandmother, and she was here to take him back. When he came out of the building I called him. He looked, saw me, and walked to my car. We're home now. He has barely spoken a word."

"I'm not surprised, but I am surprised at what we've learned about the rag, and what we've learned is quite astonishing. Come over in thirty minutes. Kate and Masaneka are preparing sandwiches."

"Sounds good! I'll be there with Stuart in thirty minutes."

A short time passed as Kate and Masaneka prepared lunch, Grammy got Stuart to get ready to go, and Myrtle took her notes about the rag and headed back home.

Myrtle walked through the back door carrying a computer projector. "That looks great girls, thanks. Grammy and Stuart are probably on their way, and Grammy said that he's still in a deep daze. When he hears what I have to say, we may see a serious reaction, so let's stay calm while I explain what we discovered about the rag."

"Sure," both girls said.

"Did you find out anything that surprised you?" Masaneka asked.

"Did I ever, but you'll hear all about it when they get here. We'll eat after that." Myrtle headed into the living room to set up her projector, call up her findings, and then put the rag on the table next to her laptop. "What's his reaction going to be?" she whispered to herself. And with that she headed to her bedroom.

A knock came from the front door. Kate ran over and let Grammy and Stuart in. Stuart was still in a daze. Grammy walked him to a chair and told him to sit down. He just sat and stared.

"Oh good, we're all here. Let's begin." Myrtle turned to her computer and fired it up. She then brought up a screenshot on her computer. Everyone looked at it but Stuart. Kate's hand flew to her mouth. Masaneka's eyes opened wide. Grammy gasped.

Myrtle began. "Stuart," she said in a strong voice. He did not look up. "Stuart," she said in a louder voice. He looked up, confused. "Please keep your eye on the screen. Will you do that?"

He nodded.

"First, my colleagues and I have found that the rag is not a rag but instead some kind of flexible material which we have no example of here on Earth." She paused. "Second, we tried to cut a piece, and we could not cut it. Third, we tried to burn it, and again, nothing as it did not burn. Fourth, we put it under an electron microscope, and we saw that it is not a fabric at all, but we also don't know what it is. Lastly, after analysis with the electron microscope, we believe that it is made of an element that does not exist in the Periodic Table of the Elements. It is not from our solar system."

She walked over to Stuart.

"Stuart," she said loudly. He looked up at her as she said in a very strong and emphatic voice, "This rag upon which we spent the entire morning using all the equipment available to us, we have concluded that it is from another galaxy. Stuart, you were on an unidentified anomalous phenomenon. You were on a flying saucer!"

"I know," he said in a soft voice. "I know." He shook his head. "They gave me the rag as a gift. They probably didn't see it as a rag. They told me they are here in peace; they do not have wars on their planet. They live in peace." Peace.

Bibliography

Chasan, Aliza, "The story behind the "Tic Tac" UFO sighting by Navy pilots in 2004, https://www.axios.com/2024/02/08/ufo-uap-sightings-us-hotspots-2000-2023

Costa, Cheryl and Linda Miller Costa, "UFO Sightings Desk Reference United State of America 200—2015, Dragon Lady Media, LLC, 2017

DiGiammerino, Thea, Published June 29, 2023; updated on 6/29/2023

"Ex-official who revealed UFO project accuses Pentagon of 'disinformation' campaign," mmoz-extension://7d247936-901d-4374-819f-6d38897111033 pages/

"Experts Weigh In on Pentagon UFO Report," https://www.scientificamerican.com/article/experts-weigh-in-on-pentagon-ufo-report/

Fitzpatrick, Alex and Erin Davis, "America's UFO hotspots, mapped," https://www.axios.com/2024/o2/08/ufo-uap-sightings-us-hotspots-2000-2023

"Government Report Finds No Evidence U.F.O.s Were Alien Spacecraft." Moz-extension://7d247936-901d-4374-819f-6d3889711033/pages/

Graff, Garrett M., "UFO The Inside Story of the US Government's Search for Alien Life Here-and Out There," Avid Reader Press, 2023.

Graves, Ryan, "We Have a Real UFO Problem. And It's Not Balloons." https://www.politico.com/news/magazine/2023/02/28/ufo-uap-navy-intelligence-00084537.

Government Report Finds No Evidence U.F.O.s Were Alien Spacecraft.

Kean, Leslie, "UFOs, Generals, Pilots, and Government Officials Go on the Record," Harmony Books, 2010.

Milburn, Franc, "The Pentagon's UAP Task Force," Mideast Security and Policy Studies No. 183, Bar-Ilan University, 2020.

"Mysteries Decoded UFO Expert Ryan Sprague on extraterrestrials and what they may want from us," moz-extension://7d247936-901d-4374-819f-6d3889711033/pages/...

NARCAP Technical Report B, Appendix A, "A Brief Overview of the Recent History of UFO/UAP Observations."

O'Leary, Abigall. "Wormhole of flashing lights over UFO hotspot island baffles scientists." Mirror.

Pentagon UFO videos," https:/enm/Wikipedia.org/wiki/Pentagon_UFO_videos

"Pentagon now reports about 400 UFO encounters: 'We want to know what's out there."

"Preliminary assessment: Unidentified Aerial Phenomena," Office of the Director of National Intelligence, 25 June 2021.

Tingley, Brett. "New Details Emerge On The "Highly Modified Drone" That Outruns Police Helicopters Over Tucson." June 1, 2021.

"The Reference Shelf, Exploring Contemporary Issues with Selected Primary & Secondary Sources." Grey House Publishing, Amenia, New York, 2022.

Pendlow, Gregory W., an Donald E. Welzenbach. The CIA and the U-2 program, 1954-1974. Central Intelligence Agency, 1998, pp.72-73, "U-2s, UFOs, and Operation Blue Book." https://www.history.navy.mil/browse-by-topic/disasters-and-phenomena/u2s-ufos-operation-blue-book-html

"Watch USS Nimitz 'Tic Tac' UFO: Declassified Video Clip

I HISTORY Channel" https://www.history.com/videos/
uss-nimitz-tic-toc-ufo-declassified-video

Wagh, Manasee, "Are Underwater UFOs an Imminent
Threat? The Government Sure Thinks So-And Here's the
Proof," August 08, 2024. https://www.history.com/videos/
uss-nimitz-tic-tac-ufo-declassified-video

"What are the UAPs, and why do UFOs have a new name?"
moz-extension://7d247936-901d-4274-819f-6d3889711033/
pages

ABOUT THE AUTHOR

Ned grew up in Framingham, Massachusetts. And after graduating from Framingham High School, he went on to Fitchburg State College where he graduated "cum laude". He also has a master's in education from Framingham State College, and a Certificate of Advanced Study from Boston University.

At Fitchburg he majored in elementary education, and after graduating he became a fifth-grade teacher at the Juniper Hill School in Framingham. He then went on to teach sixth grade at Walsh Middle School. His next position was the Director of Reading in the Sherborn, MA elementary school.

During his teaching while in Sherborn he wrote

the Teacher's Manual and the Student Workbook for the Xerox & Ginn publishing company's "Ginn 360" sixth grade reading program, and several years later he wrote the "Ginn 720" sixth grade reading program. These two series consisted of a Teacher's Manual, a Student Workbook, and an accompanying Language Arts "Skillpak."

He then went on to be the Director of Special Education in Stow, MA., where his program was rated one of the top ten in the state for its implementation of Chapter 766. He then had a dual position in Stow as Hale School Principal and Director of Special Education. His final position in education was as principal of the Willard School in Concord, Massachusetts.

From education he went on to high tech working for Digital Equipment Corporation where he held several different positions from manufacturing to international marketing. In his position as marketing coordinator for the launch of the largest software product at that time, he launched the product first in the United States, and then, two months later, in 1991, in Paris, at the first meeting in the history of Europe when the Ministers of Defense of Europe met for peacetime reasons. The product was designed to write the software code for very large planes, ships and submarines. The product had in it a software code strategy that would detect any new code written based on the previously written code that might conflict with that previously written code. It was of course much more technical than that.

From Digital Ned went into international sales training and consulting with the Harvard Research group and then Achieve Global, retiring from Achieve Global in 2002.

After his two youngest children married, he sold his home in Southboro, Massachusetts. and moved to Westport, Massachusetts.

There he became a member of the Friends of the Westport Free Public Library and the Westport Cultural Council, and from both organizations he made many friends and played a role in seeing many impressive projects, programs and staff evolve with the wonderful teams of people in these two organizations and the many projects and programs that were supported by staff and by significant financial support.